Firefighters to the Rescue!

by Judy Katschke
illustrated by Clare Elsom

Scholastic Inc.

"It's Fire Safety Week!" Julia said.
Every kid in Ms. Fickle's class had a
special fire safety project.
Wait till everyone sees my fire helmet,
Josh thought. *It's hot stuff!*

Ms. Fickle dressed up as someone new every day.
Today she was a firefighter.
"Meet Blaze," Ms. Fickle said. "He's a real firehouse dog!"

Suddenly—*WHIRRRRR*—the bell rang.
"This is a fire drill," Ms. Fickle said.
"Everybody line up and follow me
outside."

Ms. Fickle led the kids outside.
There was no fire, but there was a
fire engine.
And real firefighters, too!

"Kids, I have a surprise for you,"
Ms. Fickle said. "Chief Martinez
is coming to see your fire safety
projects."
Wait till he sees my helmet, Josh
thought. *I'll be the fire safety superstar!*

NIBBLES

Back in the classroom, Ms. Fickle
turned to the kids.
"Who wants to go first?" she asked.
"Me, me!" Josh shouted. "Pick meee!"

"Why don't you go first, Colin?"
Ms. Fickle asked.
Josh put his hands down.
What does Colin have that could be better than my fire helmet? he thought.

Colin stood up in front of the class. "If your clothes are on fire," Colin said, "the best thing to do is stop, drop, and roll!"

STOP, DROP, ROLL!

Colin dropped to the floor and rolled fast, faster, fastest!
Chief Martinez smiled.
"And remember, if there's a fire, don't hide—go outside," the chief said.

Josh was worried.

Colin's fire safety tip was really neat!

All I have is a fire helmet, Josh thought sadly. *Boring!*

"Who's next?" Ms. Fickle asked. Josh was glad when Kono said, "I'll go next, Ms. Fickle!"

Kono rocked out with a song about fire safety:

"When there's a fire and you need help to come, pick up a phone and call 911!"

The kids cheered for Kono.
Then Chief Martinez added:
"Remember the numbers 911,
but never call them just for fun."

Josh was worried.

Kono's song rocked!

All I have is a fire helmet, Josh thought sadly. *What was I thinking?*

"Who's next?" Ms. Fickle asked.
Josh was glad when Andrew raised
his hand.
"I'll go next, Ms. Fickle!" he said.

Andrew placed a box on the table.
Inside was a model of his house.
"In case of fire, every room should
have an escape route," said
Andrew.

Andrew put down a cheese trail to show the exits.

Everyone cheered as their class pet nibbled his way to safety!

"Nice work!" said Chief Martinez. "And remember to pick a meeting place outside."

Josh was worried.
Andrew's model was cool!
All I have is a fire helmet, Josh
thought sadly. *Not cool.*

"Who's next?" Ms. Fickle asked.
Josh was glad when Molly raised
her hand.
"I'll go next, Ms. Fickle!" she said.

Molly had a cupcake with a candle
on top.
It wasn't her birthday.
It was her fire safety project!
Chief Martinez lit the candle.
Molly put a glass jar over it.

Poof! The flame went out!
"Fire needs air to burn," Molly said.
"Good job, Molly!" said Chief
Martinez. "And remember, kids,
never play with matches."

Josh was worried.

Molly's science project was smokin'!

All I have is a fire helmet, Josh thought sadly. *What a snooze.*

"Who's next?" Ms. Fickle asked.
Josh was glad when Julia raised her
hand.
"I'll go next, Ms. Fickle!" she said.

Julia wrote a story for her project. "Once upon a time, Princess Sparks stopped a fire-breathing dragon from burning down the kingdom," Julia read. "And they all lived safely ever after!"

"Great story!" said Chief Martinez.
"And remember, if there's a real fire,
always call the firefighters."

Julia's story about fire safety was epic. *All I have is a fire helmet,* Josh thought. "Josh, would you like to go next?" Ms. Fickle asked. "Um . . . I forgot my project, Ms. Fickle," Josh said.

But Blaze ran over and pulled Josh's fire helmet out of his bag!
"That's a real fire helmet!" the chief said. "Where did you get it?"
"From my aunt," Josh said. "She's a firefighter."

"Josh, your aunt is a firefighter?"
Ms. Fickle asked.
"Awesome!" Andrew exclaimed.
"I want to be a firefighter!" Kono said.
"Like Josh's aunt!"

"A firefighter's helmet is important, kids," Chief Martinez explained. "It protects us from heat and falling stuff." He gave Josh a high five. "Great job!"

I guess my project was hot stuff after all, Josh thought.

Chief Martinez led the class outside. Everyone got to go inside his fire engine.

"Thanks, Chief!" the class cheered. The fire chief smiled. "Remember: Fire safety protects you and me!"